The Little
Treasu

Collections for exploration and investigation

Written by
Pat Brunton and Linda Thornton
Edited by Sally Featherstone

Photographs by alc

Little Books with **BIG**ideas®

The Little Book of Treasureboxes®

ISBN 1 905019 49 1
978 1 905019 49 6

© Featherstone Education Ltd, 2007
Text © Pat Brunton and Linda Thornton, 2006
Illustrations © alc, 2006

Series Editor, Sally Featherstone

First published in the UK, February 2006

Little Books is a trade mark of Featherstone Education Ltd

Treasureboxes® is a registered trademark of alc associates ltd, covering publications, training, and resources

Published in the United Kingdom by
Featherstone Education Ltd
PO Box 6350
Lutterworth LE17 6ZA

Printed in the UK on paper produced in the European Union from managed, sustainable forests

Contents

Introduction

What is a Treasurebox?

A Treasurebox is a collection of themed resources carefully chosen to engage children's attention, encourage their curiosity, and spark their imagination. Treasureboxes are designed to provide starting points for young children's investigation and exploration of the world around them, building on their own ideas and understanding. The ideas in the Little Book of Treasureboxes can be used with children in the Early Years Foundation Stage, but are also useful for transition into Key Stage 1.

In this book we introduce the idea of using Treasureboxes by looking in detail at how you might use four different Treasurebox collections:

> the Tool Box
> the Natural Box
> the Shoe Box and
> the Toy Box.

Treasureboxes pose questions and invite children to investigate and explore. By presenting collections of everyday objects in new and different ways you can use Treasureboxes to stimulate children's curiosity, creativity and communication - finding the extraordinary in the ordinary.

Children's curiosity about the world around them is evident from the day they are born. From a very early age babies use all their senses to explore themselves and their surroundings in their efforts to make sense of the world. Long before they can talk they are clearly investigating, asking questions, problem solving and making choices as they play, eat, and interact with others around them.

As children grow they are constantly adding to their store of knowledge about the world. Every new experience, wherever it takes place - indoors, outdoors, in the home or in the early years setting - presents a new learning opportunity.

In very young children curiosity is largely impulsive as they are attracted to new and interesting things. They express their interest through all their senses by asking 'What does it look like?', 'What does it feel like?' 'What does it sound, taste or smell like?' As they get older their curiosity becomes more focused as they start to look for reasons and explanations for why things happen.

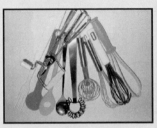

As adults we all have a responsibility to support and reinforce this innate curiosity, and to give children the confidence to develop their own theories about the world and how it works. Children need opportunities to find out about themselves, significant people in their lives, their immediate environment and the natural and man made world.

Research has identified 'sustained shared thinking' as a vital element in learning, and we have a responsibility to work sensitively alongside children as they explore and experiment, hypothesise and test their theories about the world. Sustained shared thinking is described as:

'An episode in which two or more individuals 'work together' in an intellectual way to solve a problem, clarify a concept, evaluate activities, extend a narrative etc. Both parties must contribute to the thinking and it must develop and extend.'
(EPPE)

and it is at the heart of the work described in this book.

Treasureboxes are collections of what may appear to us as adults to be very ordinary objects. But, presented in new ways, and in unusual situations they are an ideal starting point for stimulating curiosity and developing wonderful ideas.

When would you use a Treasurebox?

You can incorporate the use of Treasureboxes in both short and long term planning processes you have adopted in your setting or school. Using Treasureboxes you will also be able to plan for the needs of children of different ages and stages of development.

Treasureboxes can:
* * be central to a topic
* * support a theme
* * enrich everyday experiences.

Incorporating Treasureboxes in Topic based planning

Many settings plan for 6 topics per year, one every half term. For example you may choose to plan for the following topics in a year:

Autumn Term:	In Autumn	Our Toys
Spring Term:	Food We Eat	Living Things
Summer term:	Clothes we Wear	At the Seaside

You could use your Treasurebox collections as a focus for these topics:

Autumn Term:	A Natural Box (Autumn)	A Toy Box (Toys)
Spring Term:	A Tool Box (Food)	A Natural Box (Living Things)
Summer term:	A Shoe Box (Clothes)	A Natural Box (Seaside)

Incorporating Treasureboxes in Theme based planning

Throughout the year, some themes or strands of learning recur regularly. Treasureboxes can be used to support themes which are of particular interest to children, or which develop specific skills and understanding. Here is an example

of three common themes and the Treasureboxes you could use to provide opportunities for discovery.

How things work:	A Toy Box, A Tool Box
Looking closely:	A Natural Box, A Tool Box
Making things:	A Shoe Box, A Toy Box

Planning from everyday opportunities

Treasureboxes can be used to enrich the children's day to day experiences by providing stimulating resources to engage their attention and encourage curiosity and communication. Using your Treasureboxes for free play and exploration will expand their use even further.

You could also use Treasureboxes to support different activities in your setting:

In water and sand play:	A Toy Box
In role play and storytelling:	A Shoe Box
In cooking:	A Tool Box
During outdoor play:	A Natural Box
In small world play:	A Toy Box

Making a Treasurebox

Putting together a Treasurebox can be a worthwhile activity in itself which can involve the children, their parents and the other adults in your setting. Putting the collection together can provide important learning opportunities when you can can target particular aspects of the curriculum that you want to focus on, using the opportunities to develop children's interests and encourage family involvement in children's learning.

Further information on putting together a Treasurebox collection can be found on pages 8 and 9.

The initial stimulus for making a Treasurebox might be:

Adult led: starting from a small selection of items which you have chosen as a focus;

Child initiated: arising from the children's interest in a special object or event;

Family supported: based on a desire to involve family members in creating and using collections.

Adult led Treasureboxes

If you decide to link your collection to a theme or topic, you are likely to have specific learning objectives in mind which will influence what you decide to include in your Treasurebox. You could either put together the whole collection yourself, or begin by creating a small collection which can be added to by the children.

For example:

A Tool Box will encourage the children to investigate how things work and what they do. It will inspire them to ask questions, seek explanations and carry out investigations.

In your Tool Box you might include: a wooden spoon, a rotary whisk, a pair of chopsticks, a sieve, a rolling pin and some measuring spoons.

This forms the core of your collection, to which the children might add: a garlic press, a ladle, some tongs, a balloon whisk, pastry cutters or a knife and fork.

Child initiated Treasureboxes

It is always important to maintain a balance between adult led and child initiated learning opportunities, and the DfES is now suggesting that the balance should be equal. Using the Treasurebox approach will help you to be flexible and to respond to the enthusiasms of the children by allowing them to build up their own collections of things which interest them.

For example:

A Toy Box collection, perhaps initiated by a child bringing in a special birthday toy, might focus on developing an understanding of the past and how things have changed.

Toys belonging to older brothers and sisters, parents and grandparents will stimulate discussion about play, games and family life in times gone by.

Family Treasureboxes

Treasureboxes can be used as a focus for involving families in the life of your setting and are an enjoyable way of encouraging family members to support their children's learning. Helping to create and maintain your Treasureboxes, will encourage parents and other family members to develop their own skills and knowledge, and to benefit from the social interaction they have with other families and staff.

For example:

Putting together a Shoe Box collection provides an ideal opportunity to explore multicultural issues and gain a shared understanding of different cultures and

beliefs. Being involved in helping to put together a Treasurebox collection parents and carers will also gain an understanding how and why treasure boxes are used in your setting.

Once established, you may wish to set up a lending library of Treasureboxes so that children and their families can explore, investigate and discover together at home.

Asking questions

Using Treasureboxes in your setting will help to develop a climate for curiosity, where children are confident to ask questions, seek explanations and develop their critical thinking and problem solving skills.

To encourage children to ask questions it is important to:
* provide them with lots of **opportunities**;
* show, by your reaction and your body language, that you **value** their answers;
* give children **time** to think and to respond - don't fill the silences;
* **listen** to children's answers before framing the next question;
* **model** a questioning mind by thinking out loud and asking good questions yourself - 'I wonder why...?', 'What would happen if...?'.

What sorts of questions should we ask?

Questions can be divided into two broad groups, closed questions and open questions.

Closed questions have a right and a wrong answer. For example:

    'How many pairs of shoes can you find?'

    'Which spoon is the biggest?'

Closed questions test children's knowledge, and they do have a value in that they help children to recall and review information that they already have.

Open questions don't have one word answers, instead they encourage children to express their opinions, explore and investigate and transfer knowledge gained in one situation to help to solve problems in another.

Some examples of problem posing questions are:

    'Can you find a way to...?'

    'Why do you think... does that?'

If the focus of the question is person centred - 'What do YOU think?' children will be more willing to offer an opinion.

What sorts of questions are the most useful?

Questions which follow the children's interests and ideas.

Questions which have more than one possible answer, and which encourage further investigation.

Real questions to which you yourself do not know the answer. These encourage shared ideas, explorations and discoveries.

Scientific knowledge and understanding is divided into seven key areas:

- living things
- materials
- air, atmosphere and weather
- structure of the earth
- earth in space
- forces
- energy.

Knowledge and understanding within design technology includes:

- materials
- energy
- structures
- control.

History (a sense of time) has three aspects:

- change over time
- accounts of like in the past
- investigating the traces of the past which remain.

Geography (a sense of place) is the study of:

- places
- people
- environments.

Reading these descriptions will help you to understand how varying the contents of a Treasurebox can help you to focus on any one of these aspects of the early years curriculum, and the goals they include.

The Spiral of Discovery

The activities described in the Little Book of Treasureboxes have been set out to demonstrate the Spiral of Discovery based on the word TREASURE.

T heme or Topic

R esources

E xploring

A sking questions

S eeking

U nderstanding

R eflecting

E valuating

The **five stages** in this Spiral are:

Exploring

Asking questions

Seeking understanding

Reflecting

Evaluating

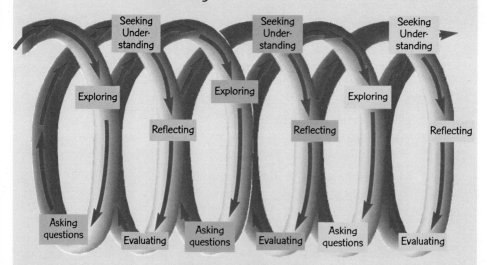

As the children move through the Spiral of Discovery and reflect on what they have discovered new ideas emerge, leading to new explorations.

Using the book

The Little Book of Treasureboxes is divided into four sections, the Tool Box, the Natural Box, the Shoe Box and the Toy Box.

Each section begins with a description of the basic contents of the box and then lists the six different themes you can explore using the resources in the box.

On the six themed pages:

The '**Page title**' describes the particular focus of the investigations and explorations.

'**What you need to collect for this investigation**' lists the individual objects from the Treasurebox collection that you will need to explore this theme.

'**Exploring and Asking Questions**' is the starting point for the children's explorations. It is the part of the process where '**sustained shared thinking**' begins. It also includes examples of questions you might ask to focus the children's attention as well as ideas for investigations that the children might suggest.
Remember to build on the children's interests and experience by following up on as many of these ideas as possible. This will involve genuine shared thinking between you and the children, and may mean that the investigation takes a different path from the one suggested in the text.

'**Seeking Understanding**' takes one of the possible questions and develops it in more detail. This provides the opportunity to plan, carry out and record an investigation and illustrates some of the important principles to be taken into account. It is ONLY ONE route you could take, not a suggestion that adult directed activities should over-ride the children's own ideas!

'**Reflecting and Evaluating**' suggests questions you might use to help the children review their investigations and discoveries as well as offering starting points for new explorations. Use this as an opportunity to develop children's critical thinking and problem solving skills.

Finally, '**Key words**' are included to extend the children's vocabulary and introduce useful technical language.

The Tool Box

The Tool Box Treasurebox is a collection of kitchen utensils with different structures, properties and functions. The collection enables children to think about why we use tools, to investigate how simple tools work and to begin to explore forces.

What you need to collect for the Tool Treasurebox activities

* tools for mixing, stirring and whisking, including a variety of forks, spoons and whisks
* sieving and separating tools including funnels, sieves, strainers and a slotted spoon
* a collection of tools with holes in, used for different purposes, for example a colander an egg timer and a spaghetti measure
* a selection of shiny tools which you can see you reflection in, for example spoons, ladles and metal bowls
* tools which we use to squash and shape things, including a rolling pin, a garlic press and a lemon squeezer
* a collection of spoons from different parts of the world, for example rice spoon, bamboo ladle and souvenir spoons

More detail of what to include in your collection is given in the Resources section linked to the six different themes.

The Little Book of Treasureboxes

Free Exploration

The complete Tool Box collection, stored in its own Treasurebox, will itself be an interesting resource to explore with the children. There will be opportunities for observing closely, sorting, classifying and using descriptive language, all important parts of the investigative processes of science.

The Investigations

The six themes in this section of the Little Book of Treasureboxes are:

- Mixing and whisking
- Sieving and separating
- Holes
- Shiny surfaces
- Squeezing, squashing, shaping
- Spoons around the world.

For each theme you will need to use a small range of tools from your complete Treasurebox collection.

Choosing investigations and responding to questions

? During the 'Exploring and Asking Questions' phase the children will come up with all sorts of different questions about what they would like to know. Some of these possibilities are included in the book, but the children will come up with many more good ideas relating to their interests and prior experience. These ideas could form the basis of interesting and enjoyable further investigations to carry out with the children.

? You may choose to use the example of an investigation included in the section 'Seeking Understanding' with one group of children while others investigate some of the other questions they have come up with.

? The 'Reflecting and Evaluating' section suggests some starter questions to help the children review what they have discovered. In some instances this will include evaluating what they have done and thinking about how they might do things differently in the future.

? At the end of each investigation, you will find new ideas and possibilities for further investigations.

The Tool Box
Mixing and whisking

'Mixing and whisking' is an opportunity to look at simple mechanisms and to begin to explore how forces are used to make tools work.

What you need to collect for this investigation
A collection of tools used for mixing, stirring and whisking. These could include:
* mixing spoons made of metal, wood and plastic, large forks
* balloon whisks of different sizes and made of different materials: metal, plastic and wood
* hand held rotary whisk
* small battery operated hand whisk
* a set of gears such as Lego Fun Time Gears
* bubble mixture (see recipe at back of book)
* several bowls or shallow trays

Exploring and asking questions

Look at your collection of mixing tools with the children. Talk about what shape they are and what they are made of.

? Do you have any mixing spoons like these at home?

? Why do you think the whisks have holes in them?

? What happens when you turn the handle of the whisk?

? What makes the battery whisk work?

Help the children to think of some questions about mixing and whisking which they could investigate. They might ask:

? Which is the best tool for mixing flour and water together?

? What sort of sounds do the different spoons and whisks make when you tap them on a saucepan?

? Can I use the gear set to make something which turns like the rotary whisk?

? Which whisk is best for whisking up bubble mixture?

You could go on to investigate any of these questions with the children. The next section shows how you could investigate <u>just one</u> of these ideas in more detail.

> Remember to build on children's interests and experiences by following up on as many of their ideas as possible. This will involve <u>genuine shared thinking</u> between you, and may mean that the investigation takes a different path from the one suggested in the text!

Seeking understanding

Here is an example of how you might look more closely at: **Which whisk is best for whisking up bubble mixture?**

👁 With the children look carefully at your collection of whisks and discuss how each one works. Where does the energy come from to make the different whisks work?

👁 Ask the children to predict which whisk they think will be the best. To do this you will have to agree what best means. Is it:

The one that gives the biggest pile of bubbles?

The one that works the quickest?

The one that is easiest to use?

The one that needs the least effort?

👁 When you have agreed what the 'best' will be, and how you will measure this, you are ready to test the whisks.

👁 Help the children to try out all the whisks and see if their predictions were correct.

Encourage sustained shared thinking.

Reflecting & evaluating

Does it matter who does the whisking?

✓ Can you think of another way of creating a pile of bubbles?

Other questions to investigate:

✓ What happens if you turn the handle of the rotary whisk in the other direction?

✓ If I tap a metal or a plastic spoon on a table what sound does it make?

Key words

mix	soap
whisk	sphere
stir	energy
turn	
gear	
handle	
cog	
teeth	
bubble	

The Tool Box
Sieving and separating

'Sieving and separating' is an opportunity to look at similarities and differences and explore how things work.

What you need to collect for this investigation

A collection of tools for sieving and separating including:

* flour sieve, tea strainer, spoons with holes in, colander
* muslin bag (used for jam making)
* flour dredger
* plastic funnels of different sizes
* large and small tongs and tweezers; child size knife, fork and spoon, chopsticks
* a selection of small bowls and containers to hold the separate items of the mixture
* a mixture made up of 'ingredients' of different sizes. Try using sand, sugar, rice, lentils, dried peas, dried beans

Exploring and asking questions

Encourage the children to look closely at the collection of sieves and separating tools.

? Which ones have holes and which ones don't?

? Are all the holes the same size?

? Does the muslin bag have holes in it?

? What do we use chopsticks for?

Help the children to think of some questions about sieving and separating which they could investigate. They might ask:

? What happens if you turn the funnels upside down?

? Which tweezers do you think would be best for picking up lentils, the large ones or the small ones?

? How can we separate out all the different ingredients in the mixture?

You could go on to investigate any of these questions with the children. The next section shows how you could investigate <u>just one</u> of these ideas in more detail.

> Remember to build on children's interests and experiences by following up on as many of their ideas as possible. This will involve <u>genuine shared thinking</u> between you, and may mean that the investigation takes a different path from the one suggested in the text!

Seeking understanding

Here is an example of how you might look more closely at: How can we separate out all the different ingredients in the mixture?

- How can we separate out all the different ingredients in the mixture? Look carefully at the mixture of different ingredients together. Are all the different ingredients the same size?
- Look at the collection of tools and discuss what you might need to separate the different ingredients out.
- Will a sieve with holes in work better than a pair of tweezers?
- How could you separate sand from sugar?
- Is it easy to separate peas from rice? Help each of the children to choose a tool they would like to use and give them a small amount of the mixture and some empty containers to begin their separating.

Children will need plenty of time to explore this activity. Listen to their comments and conversations as they are absorbed in their investigations. Encourage them to share ideas and opinions. This is sustained shared thinking!

Reflecting & evaluating

✓ What happens when you tip a small amount of the mixture onto a shallow tray and tap the edge gently?

✓ What would happen if you added water to the mixture and then stirred it up?

Other questions to ask:

✓ Does a funnel help when you are pouring water into a bottle?

✓ Can you use chopsticks to eat jelly?

Key words

sieve	separate
strain	together
hole	apart
colander	
funnel	
tweezers	
tongs	
chopsticks	
mixture	

The Tool Box
Holes

'Holes' will provide an opportunity for children to look closely, notice similarities and differences, ask questions about how things work and develop their understanding of simple measures.

What you need to collect for this investigation

A collection of tools with holes in, used for different purposes. This could include:

* colanders - made of metal or plastic
* spaghetti measure
* tool for stoning olives or cherries
* plastic basting syringe
* egg separator, egg timer
* wooden spoon with a hole in it
* salt cellar and a pepper pot, flour or sugar shaker
* a packet of short spaghetti and a packet of long spaghetti

The Little Book of Treasureboxes

Exploring and asking questions

Investigate your collection of tools with holes with the children. Look at each of the tools and encourage them to talk about what it looks like, what it feels like and what they think it might be for.

? Why does the salt cellar have a big hole and the pepper pot have small holes?

? I wonder what happens when you pour water into the colander?

? What is inside the egg timer?

? Why would you have a spoon with a hole in it?

? Why would you want to take the stones out of cherries?

Encourage the children to think of questions they would like to investigate. They might ask:

? How does the cherry stoner work?

? How much water can you suck up into the plastic baster?

? How long does the egg timer run for?

? How does the spaghetti measure work?

You could go on to investigate any of these questions or others with the children.

> Remember to build on children's interests and experiences by following up on as many of their ideas as possible. This will involve <u>genuine shared thinking</u> between you, and may mean that the investigation takes a different path from the one suggested in the text!

Seeking understanding

Here is an example of how you might look more closely at: **How does a spaghetti measure work?**

◉ Help the children to look at the spaghetti measure carefully. Open the packet of short spaghetti and let the children look carefully at the strands. What do they look like, feel like, smell like. What happens if you try to bend them?

◉ Ask them to predict how many pieces of spaghetti will be needed to fill the smallest ring on the measure. Select enough short spaghetti to fill the ring and then help the children to count the strands to see which of their predictions was correct.

◉ Now open the packet of long spaghetti and ask the children to predict how many strands will be needed this time to fill the smallest ring.

◉ Encourage each of the children to express an opinion and then help them test the measure using the long spaghetti.

Reflecting & evaluating

✓ What else would the spaghetti measure be good for measuring?

✓ Could we measure the spaghetti after it is cooked?

Other questions to investigate:

✓ What else could we use to measure the spaghetti? Would the egg timer work?

✓ How long would it take to empty a beaker of water using the syringe?

Key words

tools	how many
metal	time
plastic	how long
wood	
hole	
spaghetti	
strand	
count	
measure	

The Tool Box
Shiny surfaces

'Shiny surfaces' gives children an opportunity to look for different reflective surfaces and to discover how their reflection changes in a curved mirror.

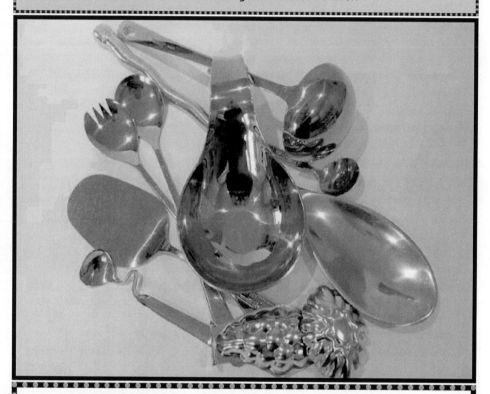

What you need to collect for this investigation

A selection of shiny tools from your Treasurebox collection. Choose tools that are shiny, and provide a reflection. Most of these will be made of metal.

* spoons of different shapes and sizes including teaspoons, dessert spoons, a cake slice, soup spoons and a ladle
* a selection of shiny serving bowls of different sizes
* metal tray, milk jug, sugar bowl or small tea pot
* measuring spoons and cups
* salad servers and large serving spoon
* butter knife or child's table knife

Exploring and asking questions

Explore your collection of shiny tools with the children. Encourage them to handle the tools and describe what they feel like, and to think about what each of them might be for.

? What do the metal bowls feel like?

? Do you have any spoons like these at home?

? What do you think we might use a measuring spoon for?

Help them to think about questions they would like to investigate. They might ask:

? Which is the best spoon for eating jelly?

? How many different shiny things can I find in the setting?

? What can I see when I look closely at a shiny surface?

You could go on to investigate any of these questions with the children. The next section shows how you could investigate just one of these ideas.

> Remember to build on children's interests and experiences by following up on as many of their ideas as possible. This will involve genuine shared thinking between you, and may mean that the investigation takes a different path from the one suggested in the text!

Seeking understanding

Here is an example of how you might look more closely at: **What can I see when I look closely at a shiny surface?**

👁 Help the children to choose a selection of different tools with shiny surfaces. Include tools with flat surfaces, such as a metal tray, as well as those with curved surfaces, such as spoons and bowls. Encourage them to look closely at their reflections in the shiny objects and to describe what they see.

👁 Do you look the same in a flat tray as you do in a curved spoon?

👁 What can you see that is different?

👁 Does it make a difference if you turn the spoon over and look in the other side? Talk to the children about their reflections, note down the words they use to describe their features in the different mirrored surfaces and encourage them to draw pictures of what they look like.

Encourage them to share ideas and opinions. This is sustained shared thinking!

Reflecting & evaluating

✓ Could we sort the tools by the kinds of reflections they give?

✓ Where else around the setting could we find things which give reflections?

Other questions to investigate:

✓ What happens when you shine a bright light onto one of the shiny tools?

✓ Will the spoons and bowls still look shiny when it is dark?

Key words

shiny	upside down
surface	
tool	
metal	
reflect	
mirror	
flat	
curved	
bowl	
spoon	
ladle	

The Tool Box
Squeezing, squashing and shaping

'Squeezing, squashing and shaping' gives children the opportunity to investigate how simple tools can help to change the shape of materials and to make some early discoveries about joints and levers.

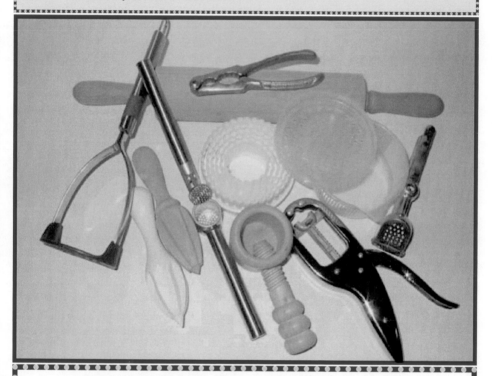

What you need to collect for this investigation

A collection of tools which we use to squash and shape things. This could include:

* rolling pin: wood or plastic
* pastry cutters: metal or plastic
* garlic presses: with different lever mechanisms
* nutcrackers: those you squeeze and those that turn a ratchet
* potato mashers: metal or plastic
* lemon squeezers: different shapes and materials; wood, plastic, metal, ceramic
* ingredients for making salt dough: flour, salt, water and cooking oil and a large mixing bowl, a tablespoon and a cup for measuring, lemon, garlic

Exploring and asking questions

With the children explore your collection of tools that squeeze, squash and shape. Talk about the different materials the tools are made of, their shapes and how different tools work.

? Does anyone have a garlic press/potato masher like this at home?

? Can you remember where else we use a rolling pin?

? What sort of shapes could we make with the pastry cutters?

? Why should you be careful when you use a nutcracker?

Help the children to think of some questions they could investigate. They might ask:

? Are there any toys which have joints and levers?

? Does a heavy rolling pin work better than a light rolling pin?

? Which lemon squeezer do you think works the best?

? Which tools will help us to make scented dough shapes?

Remember to build on children's interests and experiences by following up on as many of their ideas as possible. This will involve genuine shared thinking between you, and may mean that the investigation takes a different path from the one suggested in the text!

You could go on to investigate any of these questions with the children. The next section shows how you could investigate just one of these ideas in more detail.

Seeking understanding

Here is an example of how you might look more closely at: **Which tools will help us to make scented dough shapes?**

👁 Spend some time talking about the different stages in the dough making process and the order in which they will be carried out. Encourage the children to look at the tool collection and choose the tools they think they need for making salt dough shapes that are scented with garlic or with lemon.

👁 Help the children to measure out the ingredients for the salt dough: 2 cups flour, 2 cups salt, 1 cup warm water, 2 tablespoons oil. Mix the flour and the salt in the bowl, add the oil and then slowly add the water while mixing the ingredients. Encourage the children to squeeze, squash and shape the dough with their hands.

👁 Squeeze the lemon and garlic and mix with some of the dough. Help the children to flatten the dough and cut out scented shapes.

Encourage them to share ideas and opinions. This is sustained shared thinking!

Reflecting & evaluating

✓ Which dough do you think smells the nicest?

✓ Is it easier to flatten the dough with the rolling pin or with your hands?

Other questions to investigate:

✓ Which fruit can we squeeze juice from?

✓ What else could you squeeze in the garlic press?

Key words

squeeze	joint
squash	juice
shape	
push	
twist	
roll	
press	
force	
crush	
lever	

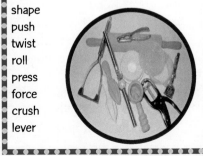

The Tool Box
Spoons around the world

'Spoons around the world' is an opportunity for children to look at tools made from different materials and to extend their understanding of a sense of place.

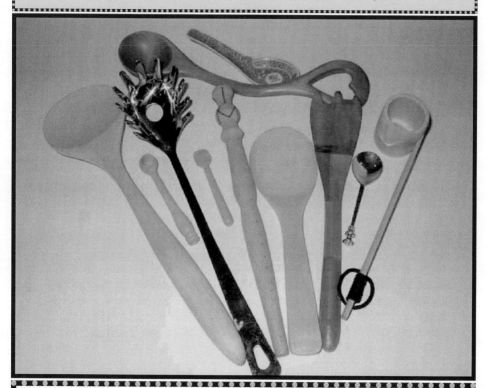

What you need to collect for this investigation

A collection of spoons from different parts of the world. This might include: Souvenir spoons made of wood, plastic, metal or ceramic, often decorated with pictures or writing to indicate where they come from. Some examples are:

* bamboo cooking spoon or ladle from S.E Asia
* rice/soup spoon from China
* Welsh lovespoon
* porridge spurtle from Scotland
* horn spoon from Scotland
* a large world map or globe, books and pictures of people around the world

The Little Book of Treasureboxes

Exploring and asking questions

Examine your collection of spoons with the children. Talk about their size, shape, colour and texture and the materials they are made from.

? Are all the spoons the same size?

? Could you use all of them for eating?

? Have you got any spoons like these at home?

? Could we sort them into those that are decorated and those that are not?

Help the children to think about questions they could investigate using their Treasurebox collection.

> Remember to build on children's interests and experiences by following up on as many of their ideas as possible. This will involve genuine shared thinking between you, and may mean that the investigation takes a different path from the one suggested in the text!

? How do people decorate spoons? Could we do it?

? Do you think any of these spoons are old? Why do you think that?

? Can we find out where the different spoons come from?

? Do some spoons feel warm and others feel cold? Why might that be?

The next section shows how you could investigate just one of these ideas in more detail.

Seeking understanding

Here is an example of how you might look more closely at: Can we find out where the different spoons come from?

👁 With the children look at the maps or the globe and help them to identify where they live. Develop this into a conversation about where different families come from and where people go on holiday.

👁 Look at the spoon collection and help the children to choose one spoon to try to locate where it comes from on the map or globe. Provide books and pictures with information about this part of the world. Repeat the process with the other spoons in your Treasurebox collection.

👁 Set up a display of your Treasurebox spoons alongside the globe or map and encourage the children's families to look at the display and talk to their children about different parts of the world. They may even have some spoons which they could donate to your collection.

Reflecting & evaluating

✓ Did you find all the places you were looking for on the map?

✓ Do you think people all over the world use spoons?

Other questions to investigate:

✓ Which spoons are the easiest to decorate? Why?

✓ How many small spoonfuls does it take to fill the biggest spoon in our collection?

Key words

spoon	globe
big	world
small	eat
find	
place	
painted	
decorate	
souvenir	
map	

The Natural Box

The Natural Box Treasurebox is a collection of natural resources which encourage children to investigate the properties of natural materials, to observe closely and to look at similarities and differences, patterns, shapes and structures.

What you need to collect for the Natural Treasurebox activities

* a variety of leaves including simple and compound leaves, pine tree needles, leaves with stripes and patterns, leaves of different colours and shades, leaves with interesting textures and scented leaves
* shells of varying shapes, sizes, patterns, textures and colours
* bark and twigs from a variety of trees, cut sections of wood and short lengths of pine showing grain and knots
* fruit and vegetables that are interesting to look at and to handle
* hand lenses and a table top magnifier
* seeds of different sizes, shapes and colours, pods with seeds still in them and cones of different shapes and sizes
* rocks of different colours, shapes, sizes; pebbles and small smooth stones of different colours and shapes; samples of sand, in varied colours and textures (graininess)

Free Exploration

The complete Natural Box collection, stored in its own Treasurebox, will itself be an interesting resource to explore with the children. There will be opportunities for sorting, classifying and using descriptive language, all important parts of the investigative processes of science.

The Investigations

The six themes in this section of the Little Book of Treasureboxes are:

- Leaves
- Shells
- Bark, twigs and wood
- Fruit and vegetables
- Seeds, pods and cones
- Rocks, pebbles and sand

For each theme you will need to use a small range of tools from your complete Treasurebox collection.

Choosing investigations and responding to questions

? During the 'Exploring and Asking Questions' phase the children will come up with all sorts of different questions about what they would like to know.

? Some of these possibilities are included in the book, but the children will come up with more good ideas relating to their interests and prior experience. Many of these ideas could form the basis of interesting and enjoyable investigations which you can carry out with the children.

? You may choose to use the example of an investigation included in the section 'Seeking Understanding' with one group of children while others investigate some of the other questions they have come up with.

? The 'Reflecting and Evaluating' section suggests some questions to help the children review what they have discovered. In some instances this will include evaluating what they have done and thinking about how they might do things differently in the future.

? Finally, new ideas and possibilities for further investigation are suggested.

The Natural Box

Leaves

'Leaves' provides the opportunity for children to look closely, notice similarities and differences and devise simple ways of sorting and classifying.

What you need to collect for this investigation

A collection of different leaves including:
* simple leaves such as beech, hazel or willow and compound leaves such as horse chestnut, ash or sycamore
* pine tree needles
* leaves with stripes and patterns - grasses, cyclamen and hostas
* leaves of different colours and shades - many varieties of house plant
* leaves with interesting textures - succulents, hairy leaves such as Stachys
* scented leaves - mint, sage, basil, parsley, coriander
* a 'sorting table' - space to lay out the leaf collection and then sort it into groups; pens and paper for labels

Exploring and asking questions

You may want to go with the children on a walk around your setting, indoors and out, to choose some leaves to add to your Treasurebox collection. This will help to focus them on what leaves are and where we find them. Talk with the children about the different features of the leaves in your collection. Help them to notice shape, size, texture, smell and pattern as well as colour.

? Why do you think the leaves are different shapes?
? Which shape of leaf do you like the best?
? Why do you think that?

Help the children to think of some questions they could investigate. They might ask:

? Do all leaves have different top and a bottom surfaces?
? Are all striped leaves long and thin in shape.
? Why do some leaves have a strong smell?
? Could we sort the leaves into groups?

You could go on to investigate any of these questions with the children.

> Remember to build on children's interests and experiences by following up on as many of their ideas as possible. This will involve <u>genuine shared thinking</u> between you, and may mean that the investigation takes a different path from the one suggested in the text!

Seeking understanding

Here is an example of how you might look more closely at: Do you think we can sort the leaves into groups?

◉ Decide with the children which feature they are going to use to sort the leaves. It is easier to start with just one feature - size, shape, colour, pattern, smell or texture. Help the children to write labels to identify each of the groups.

◉ Taking turns, encourage each child to choose a leaf to put it into one of the groups, and explain their reason:

> 'I think this leaf belongs to ... group because... '

◉ Use this as an opportunity to develop children's descriptive language as well as their observation, thinking and reasoning skills. Note down the words that the children use and take photos of the sorting process.

◉ Using the two groups you have created, help the children to think about how they could divide them into further groups.

Reflecting & evaluating

✓ What happens if we add some more leaves to our collection?
✓ Can we identify and name any of our leaves?

Other questions to investigate:

✓ How else could we sort and classify our leaves?
✓ Do the biggest plants have the biggest leaves?

Key words

leaf	pattern
plant	group
size	sort
shape	classify
colour	
texture	
long, short	
narrow	
round	
stripe	

The Natural Box
Shells

'Shells' is an opportunity for children to notice and describe shape and texture and investigate objects using only their sense of touch.

What you need to collect for this investigation

A collection of shells of varying shapes, sizes, patterns, textures and colours. This might include:

* spiral seashells - whelks, periwinkles
* shells in pairs - mussels, oysters, cockles, razor shells, clams, scallops
* limpets
* cowries
* long thin razor shells
* snail shells
* a 'feely' bag or box for investigating objects using the sense of touch

Exploring and asking questions

With the children explore your Treasurebox collection of shells. Help them to notice the similarities and differences in size, shape, texture and colour.

? What sort of creatures might live in a shell?

? What do you think the shell is used for?

? Do the inside and the outside of a shell feel the same?

? Why do some shells have spikes on them?

Help the children to think of some questions they could investigate. They might ask:

? Do all garden snails have the same patterns on their shells?

? Where in the garden is the best place to find snails?

? Are all smooth shells the same colour?

? Can I recognise a shell using only my sense of touch?

You could go on to investigate any of these questions with the children. The next section shows how you could investigate just one of these ideas in more detail.

> **Remember**
> to build on children's interests and experiences by following up on as many of their ideas as possible. This will involve <u>genuine shared thinking</u> between you, and may mean that the investigation takes a different path from the one suggested in the text!

Seeking understanding

Here is an example of how you might look more closely at: Can I recognise a shell using only my sense of touch?

👁 Help the children to decide which shells are most easily recognised using only their sense of touch. Are there any shells in your collection that are very large, very small, smooth or spiky? The simplest way to carry out this exploration is to put four or six different shells into a closed bag or box.

👁 Ask one of the children to put their hand in and feel around for a shell which matches a particular description, for example:

> the largest shell or the smallest shell
> a spiky shell or a smooth shell.

👁 As the children become more proficient you can make this exploration even more challenging by selecting up to six pairs of shells and placing one shell from each pair on the table and the other in the bag.

👁 The more alike your selection of shells is the more difficult this will be.

Encourage them to share ideas and opinions.

Reflecting & evaluating

✓ Which shape of shell is the easiest to recognise by touch?

✓ Is it easier to recognise a shell in the bag if you can look at the other member of the pair?

Other questions to investigate:

✓ How do snails move?

✓ Can you think of any other kinds of shells?

Key words

shell	same
shape	spiral
pattern	heavy
colour	pearly
smooth	
spiky	
feel	
touch	
large	
small	
pair	

The Natural Box
Bark, twigs and wood

'Bark, twigs and wood' is an opportunity to look at the textures and patterns in different examples of wood, and to investigate stability and structures during construction.

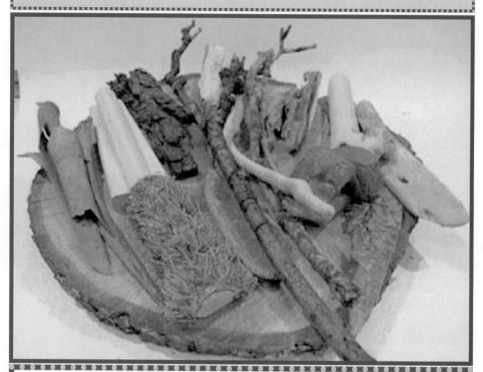

What you need to collect for this investigation

A collection of examples of wood in its natural form including:
* bark from a variety of trees: rough and bumpy - oak, ash; smooth and pattered - eucalyptus; scaly - silver birch; furry - rhus (sumach)
* twigs from different trees: different sizes, colours, shapes and arrangement of buds - ash, oak, corkscrew willow
* cut sections of wood: short lengths of pine showing grain and knots, cross sections of trees showing bark and annular rings
* paper and pens to draw a design for a bridge
* space to construct bridges and some small world animals and vehicles to test bridge models.

The Little Book of Treasureboxes

Exploring and asking questions

You may want to take the children out to have a closer look at a tree in your outdoor area, or perhaps in the car park or street immediately outside your setting. Encourage them to look at the tree, touch it, and see if they can find any twigs or bark underneath to add to your Treasurebox collection. Help the children to examine the collection of bark, twigs and wood and to look closely at shape, colour, pattern, and texture.

? Is all the bark the same?

? What patterns can you see in the cut pieces of wood?

? What shape are the tree sections?

Help the children to think of some things they would like to find out about the bark, twigs and wood.

? Do the tallest trees have the biggest trunks?

? Which type of bark is best for making a bark rubbing?

? Do all the pieces of wood float?

? Which pieces of wood are best for building a bridge?

Remember to build on children's interests and experiences by following up on as many of their ideas as possible. This will involve genuine shared thinking between you, and may mean that the investigation takes a different path from the one suggested in the text!

You could go on to investigate any of these questions with the children. The next section shows how you could investigate just one of these ideas in more detail.

Seeking understanding

Here is an example of how you might look more closely at: 'Which pieces of wood are best for building a bridge?'

👁 Help the children to plan and then draw the bridge they would like to make.
'Who is going to cross the bridge?'
'How wide will the bridge need to be?'
'How tall will it be?'
Encourage the children to select the pieces of wood they need and then use them to make the bridge they have designed.

👁 Discuss the properties of the different pieces of wood in your collection - their size, shape, how strong they are, whether they will bend or not.

👁 Record the bridge building process in photographs and note down the words the children use as they solve the problems they come up against.

👁 Use the small world play animals to test the bridge.

Reflecting & evaluating

✓ Did the bridge design work?

✓ Were our predictions about which resources we needed correct?

Other questions to investigate:

✓ Which pieces of wood would be best for making a boat for the small world animals?

✓ What sorts of creatures live in the bark of trees?

Key words

tree	colour	bridge
bark	ring	safe
twig	rough	stable
wood	smooth	unstable
branch		
log		
shape		
pattern		
texture		

The Natural Box
Fruit and vegetables

'Fruit and Vegetables' is a chance for children to look closely, notice similarities and differences and learn how to use a magnifier correctly.

What you need to collect for this investigation

A collection of fruit and vegetables that are interesting to look at and to handle including, for example:

* fruits; apple, orange, kiwi fruit, banana, pomegranate, fig, physallis; (Cape gooseberry); star fruit
* vegetables; sprout, pumpkin, carrot, leek, tomato, pepper, sweet potato, onion
* herbs and spices; garlic, ginger, lemon grass, chives
* hand lenses and a table top magnifier if you have one; *remember to keep magnifiers and lenses away from sand and other abrasive materials which may scratch the lenses*
* fine tip felt tip pens, coloured pencils and paper for drawing

Exploring and asking questions

!SAFETY! Make sure that the children understand that this investigation is about 'looking closely', and not about tasting. The fruit and vegetables are not to be eaten.

Talk with the children about the different fruit and vegetables in your Treasurebox collection. Help them to notice the different features - shape, size, texture, smell and colour. Encourage them to talk about which ones they recognise, and can name, and which ones they like and dislike.

? Why is a kiwi fruit hairy? Why are leeks white?

? Where do carrots grow?

? Does the smell of ginger remind you of anything?

? Why should we eat fruit and vegetables every day?

Some of the questions which the children might like to investigate include:

> Remember to build on children's interests and experiences by following up on as many of their ideas as possible. This will involve <u>genuine shared thinking</u> between you, and may mean that the investigation takes a different path from the one suggested in the text!

? Does a tomato look the same whichever way you cut it?

? What happens to an apple after it has been peeled?

? How many seeds does a pumpkin have inside it?

? How can I make things bigger so they are easier to see?

The next section shows how you could investigate <u>just one</u> of these ideas in more detail.

Seeking understanding

Here is an example of how you might look more closely at: **How can I make things bigger so they are easier to see?**

- 👁 Encourage the children to choose one type of fruit or vegetable that they would like to look at more closely. Help them to use the hand lenses correctly by showing them how to hold the lens at the right distance above the object and then move their head down until their eye is just above the top surface of the lens. It helps if they can rest their arm on a flat surface to keep the lens steady, or you could offer a table top viewer.

- 👁 Ask them to describe what they can see looking through the lens, and encourage them to draw a picture.

- 👁 Help the children to cut open, or peel their fruit or vegetable, to look closely at the inside.

  !SAFETY! Supervise children closely while they are using sharp knives.

Reflecting & evaluating

✓ Does the inside of a fruit or vegetable look the same as the outside?

✓ Where else do you think it might be interesting to use a magnifying glass?

Other questions to investigate:

✓ Do all fruits have juice in them?

✓ Does everybody like to eat apples?

✓ Do all apples taste the same?

Key words

fruit	bigger
vegetable	magnify
outside	lens
inside	
notice	
same	
different	
soft	
hard	

The Natural Box
Seeds, pods and cones

'Seeds, pods and cones' encourages children to look closely at shapes and patterns and to become aware of the different ways in which seeds are dispersed.

What you need to collect for this investigation

A collection of seeds, pods and cones including:
* seeds of different sizes, shapes and colours: cress, grass, wild bird seed, lentils, beans and peas
* tree seeds; sycamore 'helicopters', ash keys, acorns, beech nuts, conkers, chestnuts, fir cones
* weed and flower seeds; dandelion heads, rosebay willow herb, 'old man's beard', rose hips, sunflower seeds
* pods with seeds still in them: pea pods, broad beans, runner beans, vanilla pods
* cones of different shapes and sizes: pine, larch, spruce, fir

!SAFETY! Check to make sure all objects are safe for children to handle.

Exploring and asking questions

!SAFETY! Make sure that the children understand that this investigation is about 'looking closely', and not about tasting. **Explore your collection of seeds, pods and cones with the children. Talk about their size, shape, colour and texture.**

? Why do you think all the seeds are different shapes and sizes?

? What are pine cones for?

? Why are broad beans pods soft and furry on the inside?

Help the children to think of some questions about seeds, pods and cones which they could investigate.

Remember to build on children's interests and experiences by following up on as many of their ideas as possible. This will involve genuine shared thinking between you, and may mean that the investigation takes a different path from the one suggested in the text!

? Which pine cone smells the nicest?

? Do the biggest seeds grow into the biggest plants?

? What happens to a seed pod if it is left on a shelf for a long time?

? Can any of the seeds fly through the air?

You could go on to investigate any of these questions with the children. The next section shows how you could investigate <u>just one</u> of these ideas in more detail.

Seeking understanding

Here is an example of how you might look more closely at: Can any of the seeds fly through the air?

- Help the children to choose a range of different seeds from their collection. Discuss how you might test which to see which ones can fly through the air.

- Before they test the seeds ask the children to predict which ones they think will fly and which ones will not. Note these predictions down on a sheet so you can refer back to them at the end of your investigation.

- They could try blowing gently to see if any of the seeds can be moved by a gentle puff of air. Alternatively they could stand up and drop the seeds, one at a time, to see what happens when they fall.

- Test the seeds and help the children to record their observations on a tally chart. Help the children to check the results of their investigation against their predictions.

Encourage them to share ideas and opinions. This is sustained shared thinking!

Reflecting & evaluating

✓ Were our initial predictions correct?

✓ Which seeds can fly the best?

✓ Why do you think this?

Other questions to investigate:

✓ What do seeds need in order to grow?

✓ What happens to the shape of a pine cone as it dries out?

Key words

seed	fly
pod	wing
cone	air
shape	float
size	breeze
large	
small	
wet	
dry	
heavy	
light	
blow	

The Natural Box
Rocks, pebbles and sand

'Rocks, pebbles and sand' is an opportunity for children to explore similarities and differences and to investigate what happens when sand and water are mixed.

What you need to collect for this investigation

A collection of rocks, pebbles and sand from different places, including:
* rocks: examples of rocks of different colours, shapes and sizes, some rough and some smooth
* pebbles: small smooth stones of different colours and shapes, some showing patterns, speckles, stripes and bands. You may be able to find some pebbles which feel very heavy, or very light for their size
* sand: samples collected from different beaches which vary in colour and texture (graininess)
* a tray or table space for the children to sort and set out the collection
* small buckets or similar containers for making sand or mud pies

Exploring and asking questions

Help the children to look closely at the collection of rocks, pebbles and sand. Encourage the children to look closely using a hand lens, to touch the rocks to feel their texture and to pick up the pebbles to feel how heavy or light they are.

? Do you think all rocks feel rough when you touch them?

? Which one do you think looks the most interesting?

? Where could we find rocks and pebbles around our setting?

Help the children to think of some questions about rocks, stones and sand which they could investigate.

? Can we sort the pebbles by colour, shape or texture?

? Do wet pebbles look the same as dry pebbles?

? Which pebbles would be best for building a tower?

? Which sort of sand is the best for making sandpies?

? You could go on to investigate any of these questions with the children. The next section shows how you could investigate just one of these ideas in more detail.

> Remember to build on children's interests and experiences by following up on as many of their ideas as possible. This will involve genuine shared thinking between you, and may mean that the investigation takes a different path from the one suggested in the text!

Seeking understanding

Here is an example of how you might look more closely at: Which sort of sand is the best for making sandpies?

◉ Help the children to choose two or three different types of sand and fill a small bucket with each one. Encourage the children to investigate each type of sand in turn by feeling it with their hands.
What do you think the sand feels like?

◉ Remember to note down the different words the children use to describe the sand. Ask the children to predict which type of sand they think will make the best sandpies when water is added.

◉ Pour a small amount of water into each bucket of sand and mix it up. Then help the children to tip each bucket of wet sand out onto a flat surface to make a sandpie.
Is it important to add the same amount of water to each container to make it fair?

◉ Which one is the best? Is it the one with the best shape or the one that lasts the longest?

Reflecting & evaluating

✓ Were our predictions right?

✓ If we repeat the investigation do we get the same answer every time?

Other questions to investigate:

✓ Does wet sand help to stick rocks together?

✓ What sorts of things do we use rocks for?

Key words

rock	wet/dry
stone	stick
pebble	fair
sand	best
water	
rough	
smooth	
pattern	
texture	
mix	

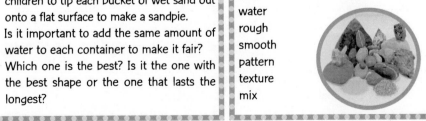

The Shoe Box

The Shoe Box Treasurebox is a collection of shoes made of different materials, from different parts of the world and worn for different purposes. This collection provides the opportunity to look at similarities and differences, sorting and classifying and investigate the properties of materials.

What you need to collect for the Shoe Treasurebox activities

All sorts of boots and shoes, such as:

Shoes for babies, children, teenagers, men and women in a wide a range of sizes, colours and materials

* shoes made of different materials, with various fastenings and patterns on the soles
* boots and shoes from different parts of the world including, for example; fur boots, sandals and clogs
* shoes and boots made of leather, rubber, plastic and fabric
* simple shoes made of a variety of materials, with different fastenings, including some shoes for toys
* special shoes with particular features - for dancing, for working, for sport

See following example pages for more suggestions.

Free Exploration

The complete Shoe Box collection, stored in its own Treasurebox, will itself be an interesting resource to explore with the children. There will be opportunities for observing closely, sorting, classifying and using descriptive language, all important parts of the investigative processes of science.

The Investigations

The six themes in this section of the Little Book of Treasureboxes are:

- Shoes that go together
- What shoes are made of
- Shoes from around the world
- Rainy day boots and shoes
- Make your own shoes
- Special shoes

For each theme you will need to use a small range of shoes from your complete Treasurebox collection.

Choosing investigations and responding to questions

? Some of these possibilities are included in the book, but the children will have many more good ideas relating to their interests and prior experience. Many of these ideas could form the basis of interesting and enjoyable investigations which you can carry out with the children.

? You may choose to use the example of an investigation included in the section 'Seeking Understanding' with one group of children while others investigate some of the other questions they have come up with.

? The 'Reflecting and Evaluating' section suggests some questions to help the children review what they have discovered. In some instances this will include evaluating what they have done and thinking about how they might do things differently in the future.

? Finally, new ideas and possibilities for further investigation are suggested.

The Shoe Box
Shoes that go together

'Shoes that go together' helps children to look closely, notice similarities and differences and devise simple ways of sorting and classifying.

What you need to collect for this investigation

A collection of shoes for babies, children, teenagers, men and women. This could include shoes for:
- babies: knitted or soft fabric, tiny trainers, party shoes
- children: sandals, lace ups, plimsols, slippers, party shoes, ballet pumps, slippers
- teenagers: trainers, flip flops, boots, canvas shoes
- men: lace up shoes, sip-ons
- women: flat shoes, high heels, boots, party or wedding shoes
- special shoes: wellingtons, dancing shoes, football boots, trainers, cricket boots

Include as wide a variety of colours, sizes and fabrics as possible.

Exploring and asking questions

Talk with the children about the different features of the shoes in your Treasurebox collection. Help them to notice shape, size, colour and what they feel like.

? Why do you think the shoes are different sizes?

? Are all the shoes the same colour?

? Does a baby need shoes before it can walk?

? Which shoe do you like the best? Why do you think that?

Help the children to think about what they could discover about their Treasurebox shoe collection. They might ask:

? How big a foot would fit into the largest shoe?

? Do all shoes come in pairs?

? Do you think we can sort the shoes into groups?

You could go on to investigate any of these questions with the children. The next section shows how you could investigate just one of these ideas in more detail.

> Remember to build on children's interests and experiences by following up on as many of their ideas as possible. This will involve genuine shared thinking between you, and may mean that the investigation takes a different path from the one suggested in the text!

Seeking understanding

Here is an example of how you might look more closely at: Do you think we can sort the shoes into groups?

👁 Jumble up the shoe collection together and then help the children to tip it out into a pile on the floor. Encourage the children to sort the collection into matching pairs. (You might want to sneak in one or two single shoes to make this more interesting).

👁 Discuss why it is important to keep shoes together in pairs. Talk with the children about some of the different features of the shoes and help them decide which feature they are going to use to sort the shoes. It is easier to start with just one feature - size, shape, colour, fastening or texture.

👁 Taking turns, encourage each child to choose a shoe to put it into one of the groups, and explain their reason:
'I want to put my shoe in this group because...'
Help the children to write labels to identify each of the groups. Take some photos.

Encourage them to share ideas and opinions.

Reflecting & evaluating

✓ Do all the shoes of the same colour fasten in the same way?

✓ Which is the most popular colour for shoes?

✓ What are the new words we have learned?

Other questions to investigate:

✓ Do the tallest people have the biggest shoes?

✓ Do any animals wear shoes?

Key words

shoe   small
foot   group
pair
sort
left
right
colour
shape
size
big

The Shoe Box
What are shoes made from?

'What shoes are made of' is an opportunity for children to look closely at the different parts of a shoe, think about the properties of materials and observe similarities and differences.

What you need to collect for this investigation

A collection of shoes made of a variety of materials, with different fastenings and with different patterns on the soles. This could include:

* shoes made of fabric, leather, plastic, rubber, wood
* shoes that fasten in different ways - laces, Velcro, elastic, buckles
* trainers with ridged soles
* slippers and boots made from fur or with fur linings
* high heeled shoes
* wellington boots
* football and other sports boots
* a flat tray of sand for making shoe prints in

Exploring and asking questions

Examine your Treasurebox shoe collection with the children. Encourage them to look closely at the different parts of the shoes and talk with them about the soles, the uppers, the lining and how they fasten.

? Are all the parts of the shoes made of the same material?
? Which shoes look most like the ones you are wearing?
? Why do you think that?
? Why do you think we wear shoes?

Help the children to think of some questions they would like to investigate. These might include:

? Which shoes are the easiest to do up and undo?
? Which shoes would be best for running around outside?
? What sort of patterns do the soles of the different shoes make?

Remember to build on children's interests and experiences by following up on as many of their ideas as possible. This will involve genuine shared thinking between you, and may mean that the investigation takes a different path from the one suggested in the text!

You could go on to investigate any of these questions with the children. The next section shows how you could investigate just one of these ideas in more detail.

Seeking understanding

Here is an example of how you might look more closely at: **What sort of patterns do the soles of the different shoes make?**

👁 With the children look closely at the soles of the shoes in your collection. Talk about the different features of the soles, whether they are smooth or rough, ridged or patterned.

👁 Encourage the children to choose one of the shoes and then press it carefully down into a tray of sand to leave an impression. Look carefully at the pattern in the sand and the pattern on the sole to see how the pattern has been made.

👁 Try the same thing with the other shoes in the collection. You could turn this into a game by asking one child in the group to choose a shoe and press it in the sand while the other children keep their eyes closed. They then have to guess which shoe made the pattern.

👁 Take some photos of the patterns and the shoes for a matching game.

Encourage them to share ideas and opinions.

Reflecting & evaluating

✓ Do all the shoes leave a pattern in the sand?
✓ Where else do you think we could make shoe prints?

Other questions to investigate:

✓ Would football boots be good for dancing in?
✓ Can you think of anywhere else where we use Velcro fastenings?

Key words

shoe	pattern
sole	shape
upper	
lining	
fastening	
material	
laces	
elastic	
Velcro	
buckle	

The Shoe Box
Shoes from around the world

'Shoes from around the world' is an opportunity for children to look at the variety of materials which shoes can be made from, to notice similarities and differences and develop an awareness of hot and cold places.

What you need to collect for this investigation

A collection of shoes from different parts of the world. This might include:
* leather boots with a fur lining inside or fur on the outside
* snow boots made of padded waterproof fabric
* leather sandals, flip flops
* embroidered fabric shoes from India and S.E. Asia
* espadrilles from Spain
* wooden sandals from Japan
* leather moccasins from North America
* clogs from Holland

Pictures, postcards and photographs showing people from around the world.

Exploring and asking questions

With the children, look at your Treasurebox collection of shoes. Talk about their shape, texture and colour and what they are made from. Look at the features of the shoes and ask some questions, such as:

? Which shoes would you like to wear if you lived in a hot place?

? Why do you think that?

? Which shoes would you like to wear if you lived somewhere cold? Why do you think that?

Help the children to think about what they could discover about their Treasurebox shoe collection. They might ask:

? Which shoes are the softest and which are the hardest?

? How does it feel if I put my hand down the end of the furry boot?

? Are the wooden shoes comfortable?

? Can we sort the shoes into those from hot countries, and those from cold countries?

You could go on to investigate any of these questions with the children. The next section shows how you could investigate just one of these ideas in more detail.

> Remember to build on children's interests and experiences by following up on as many of their ideas as possible. This will involve genuine shared thinking between you, and may mean that the investigation takes a different path from the one suggested in the text!

Seeking understanding

Here is an example of how you might look more closely at: **Can we sort the shoes into those from hot countries, and those from cold countries?**

- 👁 Look at the shoe collection, discuss the different features of the shoes and help the children to divide the collection into two groups; those they think that are from cold countries and those from hot countries. Older children could use the map or the globe to begin to identify where they live.

- 👁 Ask each child to choose one shoe and then help them to locate where it comes from on the map or globe. Provide books and pictures with information about this part of the world.

- 👁 Arrange a display of your shoe collection alongside the globe or map. Encourage the children's families to look at the display and perhaps talk about the designs of shoes people wear in different countries.

Encourage them to share ideas and opinions. This is sustained shared thinking!

Reflecting & evaluating

✓ Were our predictions correct?

✓ What sort of shoes do you think would be best to wear in this country?

Other questions to investigate:

✓ What sounds do the shoes make when you walk around in them?

✓ Why do you think it is important to keep our feet warm or cool?

Key words

shoe	fabric
boot	wood
sandal	
clog	
country	
world	
warm	
cold	
leather	
fur	

The Shoe Box
Rainy day boots and shoes

'Rainy day boots and shoes' is a chance for children to explore the properties of materials and design an investigation to see which materials are water resistant.

What you need to collect for this investigation

A collection of shoes and boots for wet, rainy weather, plus some less suitable footwear. This could include:

* rubber Wellington boots
* plastic jelly shoes
* plastic or rubber flip flops
* leather shoes
* canvas sandshoes
* some small pieces of the following materials; plastic, leather, canvas, rubberised or plastic coated material (such as plastic table covering)

Exploring and asking questions

Explore the Treasurebox shoe collection with the children and talk about the different materials that the shoes and boots are made of. Encourage the children to look closely at the shoes and feel the different textures of the upper parts of the shoes and boots.

? Have you got any shoes like these at home?

? Which shoes do you think feel smooth? Which feel rough?

? Which shoes are shiny and which are dull?

? Do flip flops protect your feet?

Help the children to think of some questions they would like to investigate using their shoe collection. They might ask:

? Which shoes are the hardest and which are the softest?

? Are Wellingtons comfortable to wear on a very hot day?

? Which shoes would be best to wear on a rainy day?

You could go on to investigate any of these questions with the children. The next section shows how you could investigate just one of these ideas in more detail.

> Remember to build on children's interests and experiences by following up on as many of their ideas as possible. This will involve genuine shared thinking between you, and may mean that the investigation takes a different path from the one suggested in the text!

Seeking understanding

Here is an example of how you might look more closely at: Which shoes would be best to wear on a rainy day?

👁 Discuss the sorts of clothes we wear on a rainy day and why we wear them. Ask the children to select four shoes or boots from the collection. Suggest they try four different materials. Encourage them to predict which ones they think will keep their feet dry and which ones will not.

👁 Look at the pieces of material, encourage the children to handle them and then help them to match each one up with one of the shoes. Talk about how you might test the different materials to see which ones let water through and which ones don't.

👁 Help the children to plan an investigation which involves dropping water onto each piece of material and seeing what happens. Is it important to drop the same amount of water on to each piece of fabric to make the test fair? Which materials soaked up the water and which ones did the water run off? Relate this back to your shoe collection.

Reflecting & evaluating

✓ Were our predictions correct?

✓ What happens if you polish the leather to make it shiny?

Other questions to investigate:

✓ Can we find any other waterproof materials around the setting?

✓ What sorts of materials are our coats made of?

Key words

shoe	waterproof
boot	inside
water	outside
wet	
dry	
leather	
plastic	
canvas	
rubber	
material	
test	

The Shoe Box
Make your own shoes

'Make your own shoes' will build on the knowledge and understanding which the children developed in 'What shoes are made of'. It provides the opportunity to introduce the children to a 'design and make' project.

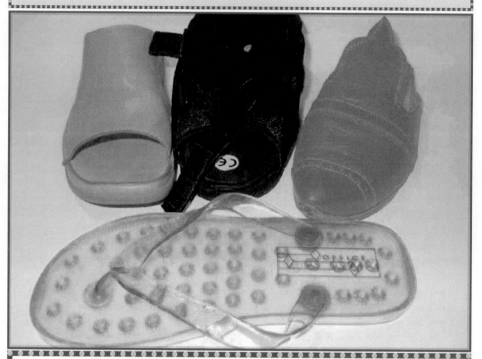

What you need to collect for this investigation

A collection of simple shoes made of a variety of materials, with different fastenings This could include:
* shoes made of fabric, leather, plastic, rubber, wood
* shoes that fasten in different ways - laces, Velcro, elastic, buckles
* flip flops and sandals
* mule slippers or shoes
* towelling bathroom slippers
* shoes for toys
* selection of card, fabric, samples of other materials, laces, Velcro, elastic, buckles

Exploring and asking questions

Examine your Treasurebox shoe collection with the children. Encourage them to look closely at how the different shoes are made and to think about why they are worn. In particular talk to them about the materials, the soles, the uppers and the fastenings of the shoes.

? Which type of shoes would you most like to make? Why?

? Who would you make your shoes for?

? How would you decide what the shoes should look like?

? What materials would you need to collect?

Help the children to think of some questions they would like to investigate. These might include:

? Which shoes are our favourites?

? Can I make my own shoes?

? Can I design and make shoes for Teddy?

The next section shows how you could investigate just one of these ideas in more detail.

> Remember to build on children's interests and experiences by following up on as many of their ideas as possible. This will involve genuine shared thinking between you, and may mean that the investigation takes a different path from the one suggested in the text!

Seeking understanding

Here is an example of how you might look more closely at: **Can I make my own shoes?**

- With the children look closely at the shoes in your Treasurebox collection and at the tools and resources you have provided. Talk about which shoes they think they will be able to make. Suggest that they could draw a design for the shoes they are going to make. They might want to draw several sorts.

- Remind them that their shoes need to be the right size for their feet and that they need to stay on when they walk. As the children make their shoes they may need to refine their ideas to make sure that they have found a way to make sure that their shoes fit and fasten securely.

- An important part of the designing and making process is the testing. Arrange a shoe fashion show where everyone shows the shoes they have made and collects comments from the group. Take some photos for a display or to discuss.

Encourage them to share ideas and opinions. This is sustained shared thinking!

Reflecting & evaluating

✓ Did the shoe designs work?

✓ How could we have improved them?

Other questions to investigate:

✓ Do the shoes in our collection have decorations on them? Could we decorate ours?

✓ Can we write or draw instructions for making a pair of shoes?

Key words

shoe	decorate
foot	pattern
size	instructions
fit	
fasten	
material	
design	
make	
test	

The Shoe Box
Special shoes

'Special shoes' will look at the special features which some shoes have and introduce the idea of using simple electrical circuits. Magic! This activity will be appropriate for the older children or those who have a particular interest in technology.

What you need to collect for this investigation

A collection of special shoes with particular features. You could include:
* shoes for dancing; tap and ballet
* shoes for working, steel toe caps and Wellington boots
* shoes for sport; golf shoes, trainers, flippers and football boots
* shoes for going out; high heels, walking boots and shoe covers
* shoes that light up; special slippers and trainers
* electrical components; bulbs, bulb holders, leads with crocodile clips attached and bicycle batteries

Exploring and asking questions

Look at your Treasurebox shoe collection with the children. Encourage them to look closely at the different shoes and to find the particular features which make them 'special'.

? Which type of shoes have you seen before? Who did they belong to?

? Do you know what they are for?

? Which shoes do you like best? Why?

? What makes them special?

Help the children to think about what they could discover about their Treasurebox shoe collection.

? Would (could you) you dance in sports shoes?

? Which shoes would you wear in mud?

? Can I find a way to make my shoes light up?

> Remember to build on children's interests and experiences by following up on as many of their ideas as possible. This will involve <u>genuine shared thinking</u> between you, and may mean that the investigation takes a different path from the one suggested in the text!

You could go on to investigate any of these questions with the children. The next section shows how you could investigate <u>just one</u> of these ideas in more detail.

Seeking understanding

Here is an example of how you might look more closely at: **Can I make my shoes light up?**

👁 With the children look closely at the shoes in your Treasurebox shoe collection which light up. Talk about other things which the children have at home which light up such as torches and radios.

👁 Show the children all the electrical components and talk to them about how the different parts work. Talk about the battery being a source of stored electrical energy Look at the bulb and talk about what it is made of. Using just the bulb and the battery ask the children if they can find a way to make the bulb light up. It will be very exciting when the first bulb lights up. Introduce the leads with crocodile clips attached and let the children discover how to light the bulb up from a distance.

👁 Help the children to secure a light bulb and holder to their shoe and make it light up.

!SAFETY! If the children wear the shoes, supervise them closely and encourage them to move with care to protect the bulb.

Reflecting & evaluating

✓ Did the shoe light up brightly?

✓ Can we draw a picture of 'how to make a shoe light up?

Other questions to investigate:

✓ How do some shoes not slip in mud?

✓ Would I paddle in puddles or swim in any of these shoes? Why?

✓ Who might wear shoes with lights on?

Key words

shoe   electricity
special   careful
dance
work
sport
light
bulb
holder
lead
battery
bright

The Toy Box

The Toy Box Treasurebox is a collection of toys which provide starting points for investigating how different toys move.

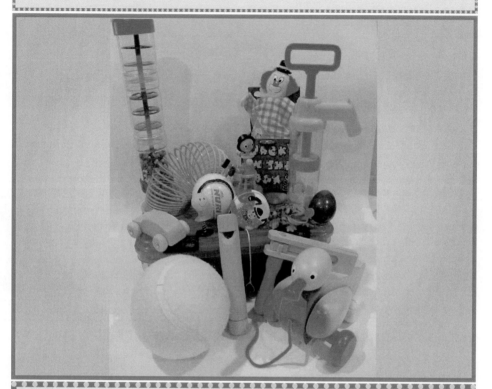

What you need to collect for the Toy Treasurebox activities

A wide collection of toys of different types, styles, sizes and contexts, such as:

* toys which you move by pushing or pulling
* toys which work by squeezing or squashing to move air or water
* toys which move by stretching or springing, using springs, elastic or rubber bands
* toys which make a noise in different ways - by tapping, shaking, blowing or squeezing
* old and new toys
* toys from different cultures and countries
* a variety of balls of different shapes, sizes and weights
* toys that float or fly or balance or spin or roll or make a noise

The Little Book of Treasureboxes

Free Exploration

The complete Toy Box collection, stored in its own Treasurebox, will itself be an interesting resource to explore with the children. There will be opportunities for observing closely, sorting, classifying and using descriptive language, all important parts of the investigative processes of science.

The Investigations

The six themes in this section of the Little Book of Treasureboxes are:

- Push and pull
- Squeeze and squash
- Stretch and spring
- Make a noise
- Old toys, new toys
- Rolling

For each theme you will need to use a small range of toys from your complete Treasurebox collection.

Choosing investigations and responding to questions

? During the 'Exploring and Asking Questions' phase the children will come up with all sorts of different questions about what they would like to know.

? Some of these possibilities are included in the book, but the children will come up with more good ideas relating to their interests and prior experience. Many of these ideas could form the basis of interesting and enjoyable investigations which you can carry out with the children.

? You may choose to use the example of an investigation included in the section 'Seeking Understanding' with one group of children while others investigate some of the other questions they have come up with.

? The 'Reflecting and Evaluating' section suggests some questions to help the children review what they have discovered. In some instances this will include evaluating what they have done and thinking about how they might do things differently in the future.

? Finally, new ideas and possibilities for further investigation are suggested.

The Toy Box
Push and pull

'Push and pull' provides the opportunity to develop an early understanding of forces and how we can make things move.

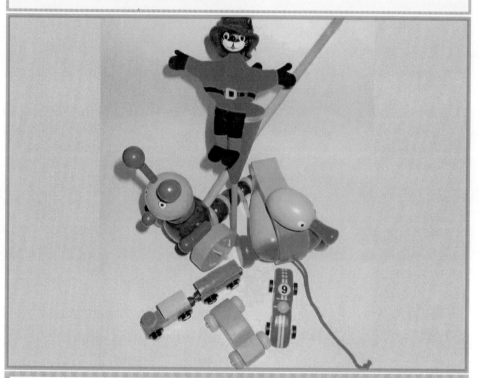

What you need to collect for this investigation

A collection of toys which you move by pushing or pulling. These could include:
* pull-along toy with string
* push-along toy with a stick
* small cars or lorries
* pop-up puppet
* doll's buggy or pram
* magnetic train set

Include as wide a variety of types, colours, sizes and fabrics as you can find.

Exploring and asking questions

With the children explore your collection of push and pull toys. Talk to the children about how they can make the toys move.

? Which ones do you push? Which ones do you pull?

? Are there any which you push and pull?

Encourage the children to talk about what they want to investigate. They might ask:

? Can I pull the pull-along toy in a straight line?

? Can I push the push-along toy in a circle?

? Which toy goes fastest? Which car goes best?

? Can I make a pop-up puppet?

? How many carriages can the magnetic engine pull?

You could go on to investigate any of these questions with the children. The next section shows how you could investigate just one of these ideas in more detail.

> Remember to build on children's interests and experiences by following up on as many of their ideas as possible. This will involve genuine shared thinking between you, and may mean that the investigation takes a different path from the one suggested in the text!

Seeking understanding

Here is an example of how you might look more closely at: 'Which car goes best?'

◉ The children will have different ideas about what 'best' means. Some will prefer 'the fastest' and others 'the one that travels furthest.' This is an opportunity to introduce to the children the important scientific concept of a 'fair test'. Help them to decide whether they are going to measure speed or distance.

◉ If they decide to measure how far the cars go, talk to them about how they will make sure that the cars are given the same chance of winning. To do this they will need to think about where the starting line is, how big a push they will give, who will do the pushing, and how they will measure the distance the cars travel.

◉ Encourage the children to look closely at the cars and predict which one they think will travel the furthest. Test the cars and help the children record their results using pictures, numbers, tallies or photographs.

Reflecting & evaluating

✓ Were our predictions right?

✓ Was the same car always the best?

✓ Was the 'push' always the same?

Other questions to investigate:

✓ Is it easier to push a big car or a small car?

✓ What happens if you push the cars down a slope?

✓ Does the colour of the car matter?

Key words

push	force
pull	furthest
best	slowest
test	
up	
down	
start	
stop	
move	
backwards	
forwards	

The Little Book of Treasureboxes

The Toy Box
Squeeze and squash

'Squeeze and squash' provides the opportunity to investigate what happens when we make air and water move, using pneumatics and hydraulics.

What you need to collect for this investigation

A collection of toys which work by squeezing or squashing to move air or water. These could include:

* frogs, snakes and snails with tongues which inflate
* balloons and balloon pump
* wooden pop-gun
* pump, syphons and syringes for the water tray
* squirting toys
* a time and place to explore the effects of squirting water

Exploring and asking questions

Choose a time and place when the children can explore the toys freely; they will need access to water to test some of the toys and space to test the pneumatic toys safely. Talk to the children about what happens when you squash or squeeze the toys.

? What happens when I squash the animals?

? Do all the toys change if they are squeezed or squashed?

? How do I make the water toys work?

Talk to the children about what is happening and help them to choose questions to investigate. They might ask:

? Why do the toys' tongues come out when I squash them?

? What happens when I stop squeezing or squashing the toys?

? Which toys squirt the best? How do I make the pop-gun work?

? Which balloons blow up the best?

> Remember to build on children's interests and experiences by following up on as many of their ideas as possible. This will involve genuine shared thinking between you, and may mean that the investigation takes a different path from the one suggested in the text!

Seeking understanding

Here is an example of how you might look more closely at: 'Which balloons blow up best?'

👁 Look at the range of balloons in your box. Talk about their colours, shapes and sizes and different ideas about what 'best' means. Is it the biggest, the fanciest shape or the one which you can blow up most quickly.

👁 Help the children to consider the original sizes and shapes of the balloons, the thickness of the material they are made from and how 'stretchy' they are. You can now introduce the crucial scientific concept of a fair test. Help the children to decide their definition of 'best' and to devise the fairest way of testing the balloons.

👁 They may decide to find out which balloon takes the smallest number of 'blows' from the balloon pump. Talk about who will use the pump, how hard they will push it, who will decide when the balloon is full and how they will record the results. Encourage the children to predict which one they think will be 'best'. Test the balloons and help the children to record their results using pictures, numbers, tallies or photographs.

Reflecting & evaluating

✓ Were our predictions right?

✓ Was the same balloon always the 'best'?

✓ Did they find a way to make sure the 'blow' was always the same?

Other questions to investigate using syringes, tubing, balloons and funnels:

✓ Can I make a toy with a tongue that works?

✓ Can I move water up and downhill?

✓ Can I make a toy that goes when I blow it?

Key words

squeeze	hydraulics
squash	syphon
pump	
blow	
squirt	
push	
best	
test	
move	
pneumatics	

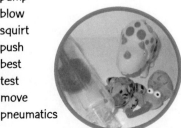

The Toy Box
Stretch and spring

'Stretch and spring' provides an opportunity for children to look at simple mechanisms and to observe how springs shorten or lengthen, and then return to their original shape after a force is applied to them.

What you need to collect for this investigation

A collection of toys which move by stretching or springing. This could include:
* a Jack-in-the-box
* toys which hang on springs
* a slinky made of plastic or metal
* 'jumping' spring toys
* a doll with stretchy limbs
* a selection of large and small metal springs

Exploring and asking questions

Have a close look at the selection of large and small springs and help the children to think about how they work. If they need help you could ask:

? Where are the springs?

? What do they look like?

? Which ones are the same and which are different?

Talk to the children about what is happening and help them to choose questions to investigate.

? What happens when the springs are squashed?

? What happens if I stretch the spring?

? Can I make a springy toy?

? How does the spring make the toy move? How far will the toys' spring stretch?

> Remember to build on children's interests and experiences by following up on as many of their ideas as possible. This will involve <u>genuine shared thinking</u> between you, and may mean that the investigation takes a different path from the one suggested in the text!

Seeking understanding

Here is an example of how you might look more closely at: 'How far will the toys' spring stretch?'

◉ The children will be fascinated by the springs in the toys and their degree of stretchiness. This activity is an opportunity to focus on children's early measuring skills.

◉ Help the children to decide how they are going to measure the toys' stretch. They will need to think about:
   Whether they will hold the toys or hang them up.
   What they will use to measure the stretch.
   How they will record what they have measured?

◉ Before they begin the investigation encourage the children to look closely at the springs in the toys and predict which one they think will stretch the furthest. Test the toys and help the children to record their measurements in the way they have chosen.

◉ Take some photos during the investigation, and when they have finished their work, talk about what they found out. Use the photos to remind them of what happened.

Reflecting & evaluating

✓ Were our predictions right?

✓ Can we explain what happened and why it happened?

✓ How easy was it to measure the stretch accurately?

Other questions to investigate:

✓ Do long springs stretch further than short ones?

✓ Which would be the best spring for a jumping spring toy?

✓ Why are springs usually made from metal? Could we make them from other materials?

Key words

spring	result
stretch	energy
squash	
move	
short	
long	
different	
same	
measure	
record	

The Toy Box
Make a noise

'Make a noise' provides the opportunity to look at a range of toys and discover the sounds they make.

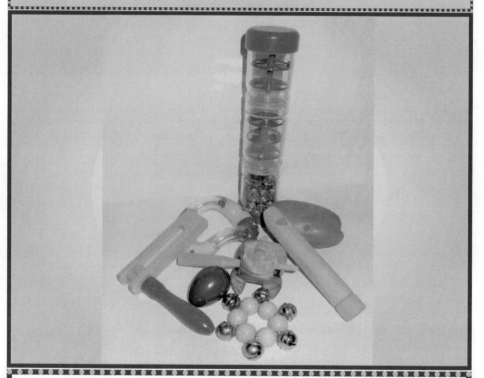

What you need to collect for this investigation

A collection of toys which make a noise in different ways. These could include:

* shakers; football rattle, *eggs*, rainsticks, babies' rattles of different designs including gourds and other rattles from a range of cultures
* scrapers; wooden frog and scraper, toy stringed instrument
* whistles; bird whistle, penny whistle
* drum, tambourine and bells
* musical box
* squeaking toys
* boxes, tubes, dowel sticks, peas, beans, beads

Exploring and asking questions

Look at your Treasurebox toy collection with the children. Encourage them to use all their senses as they explore the different ways in which the toys make a noise.

? What do I have to do to make a sound?

? What sounds can I hear?

? Are the sounds loud or soft?

Help the children to think of some questions they would like to explore further. They might ask:

? How many different sounds can I make?

? Which sounds do we like the best?

? Which toy makes the loudest noise?

? Could I design and make a baby's rattle?

> Remember to build on children's interests and experiences by following up on as many of their ideas as possible. This will involve genuine shared thinking between you, and may mean that the investigation takes a different path from the one suggested in the text!

Seeking understanding

Here is an example of how you might look more closely at: 'Could I design and make a baby's rattle?'

👁 Talk with the children about the different rattles in the toy collection- have several examples of babies' rattles if possible. With the children, explore how the rattles work and what makes them rattle. Think about the important features in toys for babies; safe, easy to hold, no sharp edges etc.

👁 Ask the children to look at the materials and tools you have provided and draw a design for the rattle they are going to make. Remind them that the rattles are for babies, and they will need to be the right size and light enough for a baby to hold.

👁 Offer your expertise as the children make their rattles - some joining tasks might be quite tricky for small hands.

👁 An important part of the designing and making process is the testing. Decide with the children how the rattles can be tested. Hopefully you will be able to find an obliging baby or toddler to do a test for you!

Reflecting & evaluating

✓ Did the rattles work?

✓ Did the baby like them?

✓ Could we have made them look or feel better?

Other questions to investigate using syringes, tubing, balloons and funnels:

✓ What other toys could we make for babies?

✓ Where could we look for pictures of baby toys to give us some ideas?

✓ What happens to the sounds if the toys are further away?

Key words

sound   make
hear   test
listen   baby
noise
rattle
whistle
squeak
loud
soft
design

The Toy Box
Old toys, new toys

'Old toys, new toys' looks at the differences between toys then and now - what they are made of, how they work and what they look like.

What you need to collect for this investigation

A collection of toys from the past, including:
* wooden cup and ball, pecking hens
* jack-in-the-box
* peg dollies
* marbles and marble games
* wooden somersaulting man
* kaleidoscope
* spinning top, whip and top
* a small selection of modern toys which the children are likely use in your setting and at home
* toy catalogues and books about toys, old and new

Exploring and asking questions

Explore your collection of old and new toys with the children and encourage them to play with them, discovering how they work. Ask the children for their opinions on the old toys.

? What do the toys do?

? How do they work?

? What are they made of?

Talk to the children about what is happening and help them to choose questions to investigate. They might ask:

? Can we invent some new games using the old toys?

? Are the old toys the same as the new ones? How?

? Are they different? How?

? What can we find out about the old toys?

> Remember to build on children's interests and experiences by following up on as many of their ideas as possible. This will involve <u>genuine shared thinking</u> between you, and may mean that the investigation takes a different path from the one suggested in the text!

The next section shows how you could investigate <u>just one</u> of these ideas in more detail.

Seeking understanding

Here is an example of how you might look more closely at: 'What can I find out about the old toys?'

- 👁 Talk to the children about how the find out about toys; from their friends, from television, shops or catalogues. Ask them to think about how they could find out about the old toys from older family members, books, catalogues or the internet. Look at the toy catalogues with the children and talk to them about how they could make a catalogue to sell the old toys in your collection.

- 👁 Encourage them to think about the things customers would want to know - for example, how they work, who would like them, what they are made of and what they would cost. Help the children to use a variety of different ways to find out information about their toys. You could use this as an opportunity to invite older family members into your setting to talk about the toys they used in the past and around the world.

- 👁 Use photos or drawings to make a catalogue of the toys. Children could dictate text for an adult to write.

Reflecting & evaluating

- ✓ Did we find out a lot about the toys?
- ✓ Was it easier to find out about some than others?
- ✓ Can we think of other ways we could have found out more?

Other questions to investigate:

- ✓ Which toys, old and new, are our favourites? Why?
- ✓ What do we think children in the past would have thought about our toys today?

Key words

old	information
new	favourite
past	
games	
different	
same	
work	
find out	
catalogue	
describe	

The Little Book of Treasureboxes

The Toy Box
Rolling

'Rolling' provides the opportunity for children to devise their own investigation using the different stages in the scientific process.

What you need to collect for this investigation

A collection of balls of different shapes, sizes and weights. This might include:
* small balls: table tennis ball, golf ball, squash ball, high bounce ball
* medium sized balls: tennis ball, dog ball, rounders ball
* large balls: football, beach ball
* balls with holes
* soft foam balls
* balls of different shapes: rugby ball, koosh ball, textured balls, juggling balls

Exploring and asking questions

Explore the collection of balls with the children. You may choose to do this outdoors where the children can explore and find out:

? Which balls roll?

? Which balls bounce?

? Which balls are easy to throw and catch?

After a period of free play encourage the children to think about what they want to investigate. They might suggest:

? Which balls are heavy and which are light?

? How far can I throw the ball?

? Do heavy balls roll best?

? Which balls bounce the highest?

? What happens if I roll a ball down a slope?

> Remember to build on children's interests and experiences by following up on as many of their ideas as possible. This will involve genuine shared thinking between you, and may mean that the investigation takes a different path from the one suggested in the text!

Seeking understanding

Here is an example of how you might look more closely at: 'What happens if I roll a ball down a slope?'

👁 This activity might build on children's experience of rolling balls along a flat surface outdoors. It is an opportunity for children to develop their understanding of the processes of science by:

deciding what to investigate

choosing the resources they need

observing closely

predicting what might happen and why

testing their ideas

recording what happens.

👁 Help the children to choose the range of balls they are going to test - different sizes, weights and shapes. Decide what sort of slope you will use - a ready made ramp, blocks and planks from the construction area or a natural slope outdoors.

👁 Remind the children about the importance of a fair test - the same slope and the same starting point for the roll. The children will need to decide how to mark the distance the balls have rolled, how to measure it and how to record the results.

Reflecting & evaluating

✓ Were we right about which ball would roll the furthest?

✓ Did we get the same answer when we repeated the investigation.

Other questions to investigate:

✓ What happens when you roll other things down the slope, for example a hard-boiled egg, a pumpkin or a gourd?

✓ Which rolls the fastest, a heavy ball or a light ball?

Key words

ball	measure
roll	slow
slope	fast
large	
small	
round	
oval	
observe	
predict	
test	
record	

Useful Information

Safety First

! When you start to build up your Treasurebox collections remember to pay careful attention to the Health and Safety guidelines which apply to your setting. Regular updates on Health and Safety are often provided by local authorities and organisations and you will find these on file along with your own Health and Safety and Risk Assessment policies - contact the Health and Safety representative for your setting.

! When selecting items to include in your Treasurebox you should apply the same criteria as you would for any other resources used by the children. They should be clean, well maintained and safe for children to handle. The variety of objects you will want to include in your Treasurebox collection will go beyond the range of everyday toys and equipment which are usually available to children in an early years setting.

! Make sure that both children and adults are aware that the resources in the Treasurebox are something special, to be used in a particular way, and not toys for everyday use.

! 'Be Safe', a publication of the Association for Science Education (ASE) is a very useful, up to date source of information for schools and early years settings.
Get a copy from: ASE Publications 01707283000 www.ase.org.uk

Choosing a box

Finding the box to put your collection in is a very important part of the whole process of creating your Treasurebox.

There is a vast range of different boxes currently available. When choosing one to house your Treasurebox collection, here are some things you will want to think about:

? What does it look like?
? Does it give any clues about the contents?
? How big does it need to be?
? How strong is it?
? How easy is it to carry?

? Is it easy to store?
? How long does it need to last?
? Will it clean easily?
and most importantly:
? Is it beautiful, exciting, magical?

Collecting your treasure

To help you build up your Treasurebox collection you may find the following list of people and places useful. Depending on your local circumstances, and the nature of the Treasurebox you are making, you will no doubt think of many others.

People who can help:

       Staff of the setting or school
       Families, including older and more distant relatives
       Committee members or governors
       'Friends of ...' association
       Local community
       Local businesses

Places to visit:

Charity shops	Souvenir shops
Craft fairs	Garden centres
Markets	Kitchen and household shops
Pound shops	IKEA
Car boot sales	Toy shops
Garage sales	Builders merchants
Flea markets	Trade shows and exhibitions
School fetes	Agricultural shows
W.I. Markets	Walks in the park, country or at the seaside

Recipe for making your own bubble mixture

       3 parts washing up liquid
       7 parts warm water
       1 part glycerine or sugar

Glycerine helps the bubbles last longer by preventing them from drying out. If you can't get any glycerine, use sugar instead.

Resources

Hand lenses, large magnifiers, mirrors and a large scale map of the world available from:

Reflections on Learning, Tonbridge, Kent. 01732 225850
www.reflectionsonlearning.co.uk

Batteries, bulbs and wires for making electrical circuits are available from:

Hands On, 01732 225800
www.handson.co.uk

Musical instruments can be purchased from:

MES (Music Education Supplies) 02087703866

Replicas of old fashioned toys can be purchased from museum shops, National Trust and English Heritage properties.

If you have found this book useful you might also like ...

The Little Book of Investigation
LB20
ISBN 1-904187-66-8

The Little Book of Science Through Art
LB1
ISBN 1-902233-61-1

The Little Book of Maths Activities
LB11
ISBN 1-904-187-08-0

The Little Book of Living Things
LB37
ISBN 1-904519-12-2

The Little Book of Seasons
LB 44
ISBN 1-905019-34-3

The Little Book of Growing Things
LB22
ISBN 1-904187-68-4

The Little Book of Outside in all Weathers
LB17
ISBN 1-904187-57-9

All available from

Featherstone Education

PO Box 6350

Lutterworth LE17 6ZA

T:0185 888 1212   F:0185 888 1360

on our web site

www.featherstone.uk.com

and from selected
book suppliers